GLORIA's BIG PROBLEM

Words by
SARAH STILES BRIGHT

Pictures by
MIKE DEAS

TILBURY HOUSE PUBLISHERS, THOMASTON, MAINE

Gloria Marvel loved to sing. Sometimes she pretended she was an opera singer.

She stood on a chair in her room, stuffed her shirt with pillows, and threw her arms all over the place while she sang in a very BIG voice. Other times she pretended she was a rock star. She stood on her bed and jumped up and down and shook her head wildly while playing air guitar.

And sometimes she pretended she was the star of a musical theater production. When she imagined this, she danced back and forth all over her room, waving her arms and making up dance steps while singing with emphasis in a nose-filled kind of way. Gloria loved to sing.

But there was a problem . . . and this Problem got in Gloria's way. In fact, Gloria's Problem got in the way of most things she really wanted to do.

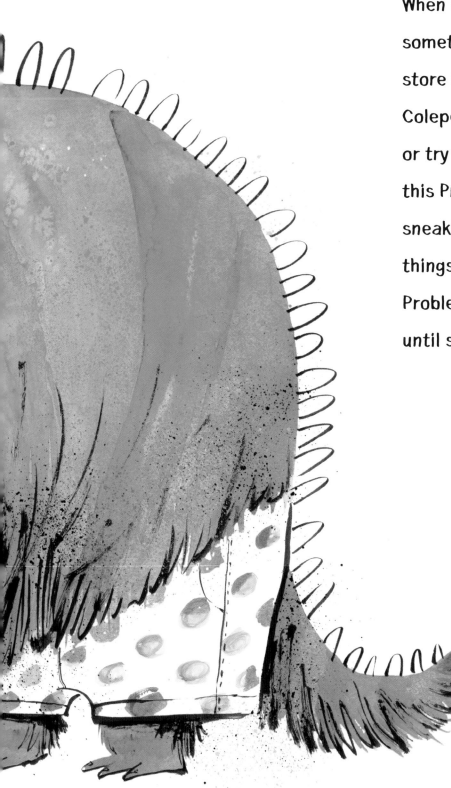

When she decided she wanted to try something, like ride her bike to the store for the first time or go to Alice Colepepper's house for an overnight or try out for the town soccer team, this Problem of hers would come sneaking around and talking about things that could go wrong. And her Problem would keep right on talking until she changed her mind.

Gloria's Problem followed her everywhere and wouldn't leave her alone, even when she asked nicely. She'd say politely, "Excuse me, but I really prefer that you don't bother me, so could you, would you, please stop making me scared?" But her Problem would say it couldn't hear her because she was speaking too softly, and then it would start speaking very LOUDLY in her ear, and it would grow BIGGER and Gloria would get very quiet and feel very small.

Once, Alice Colepepper invited her to go to the movies and then sleep over. Gloria got very excited, but then her Problem showed up and started whispering things about comets, or earthquakes, or blizzards in June . . .

TAP TAP

. . . and she decided maybe it would be better if she didn't go to the movies with Alice Colepepper after all, because what if something AWFUL happened while she was there?

Gloria's Problem could be a big pain in the neck, especially when she was singing, which, as we know, she loved to do more than anything else. And if she tried to sing in public—like at a birthday party, or in music class, or at church on Sunday mornings—her Problem would bellow in its big, unmusical, and very ugly voice, and Gloria could barely even sing in a whisper because her Problem drowned her out.

Gloria's Problem ALWAYS made her worry and ALWAYS made her feel like she was this big. The Problem could be very LOUD and very OBNOXIOUS,

PARP

THBBt!

The Problem didn't bother Alice Colepepper. It didn't bother her older brother Henry, and it certainly never bothered her parents, Thomas and Melinda Marvel. It didn't seem to bother anyone except Gloria, and to make matters worse, nobody else seemed to even see or hear the Problem. And sometimes that made Gloria feel bonkers . . . which she wasn't.

Once when Gloria tried to tell her brother Henry about her Problem, Henry laughed and laughed and told her she was nuts. That wasn't very nice.

The worst part was he was standing right next to Bitsy Snogbottom and a couple of his other friends at school, and they all started laughing at her too. Then Gloria's Problem got in her face and started her worrying about being *nuts*, and so she decided not to talk about her Problem anymore.

When Gloria heard there was going to be a play down at the community theater and all the children in town were invited to audition, she wanted to try out more than anything. So she started practicing whenever she could, even though her ridiculous Problem always seemed to be nearby making faces at her and telling her about comets and earthquakes and blizzards in June, and what the whole town thought of her singing.

The day for tryouts got closer and closer, and even with her Problem being LOUD and OBNOXIOUS and bothering her all the time, Gloria *still* wanted to sing. So she told her parents and they smiled and said, "Isn't that sweet?" and went back to their crossword puzzles.

PAT PAT

When she told her brother Henry that she was going to try out for the show, he almost fell off his chair. "You're doing what?" he howled. "You're going to get up onstage and sing in front of all those people? You can't do that! You have a Problem! A REAL PROBLEM!" He laughed some more, and then he laughed harder.

HA HA HA

Gloria's Problem (who was standing RIGHT behind her) held on to its troll-like belly and howled too, *in her ear*, so she couldn't hear herself think, but nobody saw it or heard it. And that made Gloria mad. Madder even than listening to her brother laugh. She marched out the door and down the street to the community center.

The hall was filling with parents and their children all waiting for a chance to sing. Even Frankie Fudsmutter was there (though Gloria didn't see him because he was hiding in the bathroom). Gloria looked around, knowing that her Big Problem was right behind her like it always was. She was beginning to feel the worry rise in her tummy and on up through her chest and into her throat until her ears burned hot.

She thought, "What if a tornado comes whirling through town while I'm singing and it blows me away? Or what if I slip and fall down and the whole world sees my underpants? What if a poisonous spider crawls up my leg and bites me and my leg swells up like a blimp and falls off? What if a giant meteor comes careening to earth from outer space and squashes me like a worm under a car wheel? What if there's a thunderstorm while I'm on stage AND THE LIGHTS GO OUT and I get struck by lightning and toasted in front of all those people?"

And the what-ifs kept growing and getting louder and louder and Gloria's heart raced until she thought she couldn't take it anymore. She was still mad at Henry though, and mad at all his friends who had laughed at her, mad at her parents Tom and Melinda Marvel who always smiled kindly when she mentioned her Problem but never took her seriously, and just plain mad at her Problem who always got in her way.

She was so mad that for once she stamped her feet, turned around, and looked right at the ugly troll-faced Problem and shouted, "STOP!" as loud as she could!

And to Gloria's complete surprise, her Problem shrank and hid in the shadows at the back of the auditorium.

All the children and parents in the community hall waiting to try out stopped and looked at her. The piano teacher stopped warming up. The cars outside on Gabble Street came to a halt. The postmaster over at the post office stopped sorting mail, the church choir down the street stopped rehearsing, the grocery-store clerk stopped ringing in groceries, the after-school soccer game at the ballfield came to a stop.

The dentist who was drilling Mabel Totwinger's aching tooth stopped drilling. The veterinarian stopped trying to give the Krunkles' very unhappy cat his pill. Tink at Tink's Beauty Parlor stopped trying to make Mrs. Huffstuffin's big hair beautiful. Even her big brother stopped bragging about himself to Bitsy Snogbottom in front of the movie theater. The whole town stopped . . . and listened.

Nobody had ever listened to her like that. Ever. So Gloria marched in big, confident steps up to the stage and declared, "BE QUIET! I've had enough of you, you big ugly troll!" (And her Problem shrank a little more, because if there was anything it didn't like, it was being called a troll.) "ENOUGH! Do you HEAR ME? There are no tornadoes here today and no poisonous spiders. Nobody will see my underpants and if they do I don't CARE! I am not going to listen to you anymore! You are going to listen to ME! And I am going to SING!"

And sing she did, right then and there.

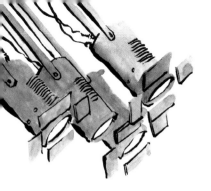

And after Frankie Fudsmutter heard
Gloria sing her heart out, he did
something he'd never done before.

He stood on a chair with his hands on his hips, looked very, very fierce, and then followed Gloria onstage, surprising everyone—most of all himself.

And later, the whole town—the piano teacher, the postmaster, Tink from Tink's Beauty parlor, and Mrs. Huffstuffin with her hair in curlers, the traffic policeman, the soccer team, the grocery clerk, the dentist and Mrs. Totwinger with her large aching tooth, the church choir, Alice Colepepper, the veterinarian and the Krunkles with their unhappy cat, her mother Melinda, her father Tom, even her big brother Henry and, of course, Bitsy Snogbottom—all came to listen. Gloria had earned herself a part in the town musical.

She was the singing ladybug with one little itty bitty song that she sang while bounding around the stage with a grasshopper played by Frankie Fudsmutter, and she sang it beautifully.

Text © 2020 by Sarah Stiles Bright
Illustrations © 2020 by Mike Deas

Hardcover ISBN 978-0-88448-739-5

First hardcover printing December 2019
Tilbury House Publishers
www.tilburyhouse.com

Hardcover ISBN 978-0-88448-739-5
Library of Congress Control Number: 2019950948

Designed by Frame25 Productions
Printed in Korea through Four Colour Print Group

15 16 17 18 19 20 XXX 10 9 8 7 6 5 4 3 2 1

Sarah Stiles Bright teaches college English and writes from Portland, Maine. She is the author of *Wind Bird*, a children's story based on Passamaquoddy legend. She lives with her Bernese mountain dog and has two grown children who are resoundingly present in *Gloria*.

Mike Deas fine-tuned his drawing skills and imagination at Capilano College's Commercial Animation Program in Vancouver, then worked as a concept artist, texture artist, and art lead in the video game industry in England and California before returning to his native British Columbia. He is the illustrator of *The Buddy Bench* (Tilbury House, 2019).